The
Adventures
of
Fog and Spangle

Presented to
Kristie Carmichael for Excellent Attendance
22nd June '03

Your word is a Lamp to my feet
and a light for my path. *Psalm 119:105*

HIGHWAY from Kingsway Communications Ltd.

© Marjory Francis

First published 2001

Scripture Union, 207–209 Queensway, Bletchley, Milton Keynes, MK2 2EB, England

ISBN 1 85999 546 2

All rights reserved. No part of this publication may be reproduced, stored in a retrieval system, or transmitted, in any form or by any means electronic, mechanical, photocopying, recording or otherwise, without the prior permission of Scripture Union.

The right of Marjory Francis to be identified as author of this work has been asserted by her in accordance with the Copyright, Designs and Patents Act 1988.

British Library Cataloguing-in-Publication Data.
A catalogue record of this book is available from the British Library.

All illustrations by Jane Taylor
Cover illustration by Jim Kavanagh

Printed and bound in Great Britain by Creative Print and Design (Wales) Ebbw Vale.

Scripture Union is an international Christian charity working with churches in more than 130 countries providing resources to bring the good news about Jesus Christ to children, young people and families – and to encourage them to develop spiritually through the Bible and prayer.

As well as our network of volunteers, staff and associates who run holidays, church-based events and school Christian groups, we produce a wide range of publications and support those who use our resources through training programmes.

*Dedicated to Kathryn, Margaret, Doreen
and Mike, the original creators
of Fog and Spangle*

Contents

Meet Fog and Spangle

Fog and Spangle are two little friends who live – well, perhaps they live down your street, and you have never noticed them! They like to do the same sorts of things that you do and their world is very ordinary in many ways, but some exciting things happen in it.

Fog is small, green and furry. His name stands for Friend Of God, and he reminds children that God wants all of us to be his friends.

Spangle is a bright yellow star. Stars have a special quality, and Spangle reminds children that each one of us is special to God.

Fog and Spangle appear in All Stars, the children's activity leaflet which belongs alongside Scripture Union's SALT 5 to 7+ material. Now you can read of their adventures, and see how, even though people may be very different, we can help each other and be very good friends.

New friends

One evening Fog was pulling the curtains across the window when he noticed something bright in the sky. He stopped for a moment and watched.

"Well I never, it's a shooting star," he said to himself. "And oh, it is coming this way!"

Fog blinked as a very bright light flashed past the window. How exciting! he thought. I've never seen a shooting star so clearly before.

In the morning he had almost forgotten about the shooting star, but when he pulled the curtains back he noticed something in the middle of the lawn. A patch of grass was burnt – and it was star-shaped! And what was more, there were little burnt footprints leading away from it!

Fog followed the footprints across the garden to the shed. He opened the door a little nervously. "Hello," he said. There was a flicker of light in one corner. "Hello," Fog said again, a bit louder. "Please come out. I won't hurt you."

An old basket in the corner moved, and a bright yellow star climbed out. "I'm very sorry. I shouldn't be here, I know," said the star. "I just wanted somewhere to rest. I was going so fast I felt I was burning up and I fell with an awful bump."

"You must have," said Fog. "Are you

hurt? Why don't you come inside? I can give you some breakfast and see to your bumps."

"Oh thank you," said the star. "My name's Spangle, by the way."

"And I'm Fog," said Fog, and that is how they met.

Fog said he would show Spangle around. Earth would be strange to a star. Before they went out to explore, Fog explained about traffic. "There are cars and lorries and buses which drive along the road," he said. "They can be dangerous."

"I've never heard of cars and lorries and buses," said Spangle. "We don't have them in space. There's just... space!"

"Well, you have to know about them here," said Fog. "You must always stop at the side of the road and look and see if one is coming – and listen too. Don't cross the road until it's clear."

"What's a road?" asked Spangle. "Why will I want to cross it? Why do you have all these funny rules?"

Oh dear, thought Fog. He doesn't understand how important it is. I'd better make sure he stays near me.

Fog took Spangle to the park for their first outing. Spangle skipped along beside Fog (he wasn't too badly hurt after all) and found everything exciting.

"There's the park over there," said Fog, pointing with his paw. Spangle could see some very interesting-looking swings across the road, and he began to dash towards them. There was a squeal of brakes, as a red car swerved and just missed Spangle. Both Spangle and the car driver were very shaken up, but fortunately no one was hurt.

"Now do you understand why we have rules about crossing the road?" said Fog, after the driver had gone on her way.

"Yes," said Spangle, "and I'll see if I can remember them this time. First I have to stop. Then I look and listen." Three more cars and a bus rushed by as they waited.

"Now it's safe, isn't it, Fog?" asked Spangle. "I'm glad you're here to help me. If I'm going to stay here, I have a lot to learn."

"Oh, I do hope you are going to stay here," said Fog as they crossed the road safely. "I have a feeling we're going to be very special friends."

Spangle found out that rules are important. In the Bible God gives us rules to live by so that everyone can be safe and happy. One day a man asked Jesus which was the most important rule to keep. There seemed to be so many of them! Jesus said that the most important ones are to love God and to love other people. You can find this story in Matthew chapter 22, verses 34 to 40.

If we ask him, Jesus will help us to live the best way.

You could say this prayer.

Please, Jesus, help me to love you and to love other people.

What's mine is yours

One day Fog said to Spangle, "Do you know, Spangle, you're my best friend."

"I thought I was," said Spangle.

"Yes," said Fog, "and I think best friends ought to share everything, don't you?"

"Yes," Spangle agreed. "Everything we have from now on, we'll share between us."

The next day, Fog had a parcel in the post. Auntie Snow had been knitting and she had sent him a warm hat. Fog tried it on. It fitted perfectly! He would wear it every day! Then he remembered the promise he had made with Spangle, so he took the hat along to him.

Spangle was very impressed. "But we can't cut it in half," he said. "We'll spoil it."

"Stop teasing," said Fog. "I wasn't thinking of cutting it in half. You can wear it one day, and I'll wear it the next."

Spangle tried the hat on. It looked very

silly on top of his pointed head, and when he pulled it down a bit he made a hole in it. Fortunately the hole disappeared with a bit of gentle stroking. "Fog, it's very kind of you to share your hat with me," said Spangle, "but it really looks much better on you."

After Fog had gone, Spangle decided to smarten himself up a bit. If Fog's looking good, then so must I, he thought. He got out his can of Star-Shine and gave himself a good squirt all over. Then he rubbed himself with a soft cloth until he was really sparkling.

That feels better! he grinned to himself. Then he remembered that he was going to share everything with his best friend Fog, so off he went to Fog's house with his can of Star-Shine in his hand.

"Fog, close your eyes! I've got something for you," he said. Fog closed his eyes and Spangle sprayed polish all over his tummy.

Spangle knew at once that it had been the wrong thing to do. Fog's tummy didn't look as if it was going to rub up nice and shiny. It looked all slimy, and was beginning to dry into messy lumps.

"Quick, Fog! We must wash it all off!" shouted Spangle. Fog jumped into the bath. There were two clouds – a pink one and a blue one – hanging from the ceiling. (Fog's bath didn't have taps.) He quickly pulled the cord from the pink cloud and lovely warm water gushed all over him. Together he and Spangle managed to get his green fur back to normal quite quickly.

"I don't understand," said Fog, as they sat down together with a drink of Sunny

Delish. "I thought it was a good thing that friends share everything."

"Yes," said Spangle. "That certainly hasn't worked for us today. But I think the main thing is that we wanted to share things. Perhaps we weren't trying to share the right things, but look at this bottle of Sunny Delish. That's something we are managing to share."

"You're right," said Fog, "and I can think of something else. I've got a bag of jelly beans in the cupboard. There's almost nothing better to share than that!"

Fog and Spangle knew that sharing what they had with each other was good, even if things didn't work out as they expected!

In the Bible there is a story about a huge crowd of people who were all hungry. One boy had his lunch with him and he gave it to Jesus. It was generous of him to share – and Jesus was able to feed all the five thousand people with his five loaves and two fishes! You can read the story in John chapter 6, verses 1 to 13.

You could say this prayer.

Thank you, God, for all you give me. Help me to be generous and share whenever I can.

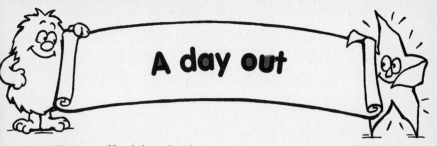

A day out

Fog pulled back the curtains and gazed out at the sunny garden. Not a day to stay in, he thought. I'll ring Spangle and we'll go out for an outing.

Spangle was a long time in coming to the phone. "I'm coming over with a picnic," said Fog. "You be thinking of a nice place to go."

"I'm not sure..." answered Spangle, but Fog had already put the phone down. In no time at all he had packed a bottle of Raspberry Rain, a bag of chocolate flavoured Hailstones and two Misty Pies, and was on his way to Spangle's house.

Spangle seemed a long time answering the door. Fog had to knock three times. He could hear a machine going inside. "That will be Spangle's Shiner," he thought. At last Spangle answered. He looked hot and bothered and he had a duster in one hand.

"I don't think I can come out today, Fog," he said. "I've got too much to do here."

"Nonsense!" said Fog. "Look, if you've things to do, I'll help you, then we can go on our picnic."

"Oh, all right," said Spangle. "The kitchen needs sorting out."

Fog came in and tackled a pile of washing-up. He enjoyed washing up at Spangle's house because the bubbles always came out star-shaped. He could never work out why, because he used the same sort of washing-up liquid and it never happened at

his home. The star bubbles seemed to make the dishes extra sparkly too.

It didn't take Fog long to have the kitchen clean and tidy. Then he looked in the fridge and found some cream cheese. Oh goody, he thought, one of Spangle's friends has been to the moon lately. He made some sandwiches and wrapped them up ready to take out. "Ready!" he called, but he could still hear the cleaner going somewhere else in the house. He went to find Spangle, who was trying to reach behind a cupboard with the Shiner.

"Oh come on, Spangle," said Fog. "You don't need to be that fussy. Let's put the Shiner away and go out."

Spangle looked unhappy. "It's all very well for you, Fog," he said, "but I keep seeing things that need doing. My sparkle shows up all the dust. Look, there's some more there!" and he bent down to wipe a tiny speck off the floor. Fog decided to be firm. He switched off the Shiner and took the duster away from Spangle.

"We're going out," he said. "Any other dust can wait for a rainy day. Come on! I've got a picnic ready!" and he almost dragged Spangle out of the door. The sun was still shining and the sky was a beautiful blue.

When Spangle saw what a lovely day it was, he gave an enormous smile. "Why didn't I come out earlier?" he said. "It's just the day for an outing. Let's go down to the stream and paddle."

"And then to the park for the swings," said Fog.

"And then up the hill for our picnic," said Spangle. "And then... oh, there are so many lovely places and so many things to do! I'm so glad you're my friend, Fog, and I'm so glad you made me come out."

Being busy and getting jobs done is good, but not if we are too busy to spend time with God and enjoy the world he has made. There is a story in the Bible of a very busy lady. She had invited Jesus to her house and was trying to make everything just right for him, but Jesus showed her that it was better to spend time enjoying being with him. You can read the story of Martha and her sister Mary in Luke chapter 10, verses 38 to 42.

You could say this prayer.

Please God, help me to enjoy spending some time talking and listening to you each day.

Spangle's birthday

It was Spangle's birthday and he had invited Fog to his party. Fog was excited. He hadn't been to a star's birthday before. Spangle had invited lots of his starry friends and it would be the first time Fog had met them.

Fog gave his fur a really good brush and hurried off with his present under his arm. (It was a round parcel – can you guess what was in it?)

Spangle's cousin Twinkly answered the door. "How nice to see you Fog," he smiled. "Let's leave your present in here. Spangle can open it when we have tea."

Fog looked at the delicious tea on the table. There were star-shaped sandwiches, star biscuits and even star crisps. Fog began to wonder a bit, especially when he put his round parcel among all the star-shaped ones.

There was quite a noise coming from the next room.

"You're just in time to join in musical stars," said Twinkly. He opened the door and Fog saw lots of stars rushing round to very jangly music. When it stopped, the stars all stood very still. This was very difficult for them as they had to try and make sure their light stopped flickering too.

"Hello, Fog," called Spangle from the other side of the room. "Join in the game!"

But Fog thought he would watch. The stars all looked very good at it, much better than he would be, and besides, they had very sharp points and he thought he might get hurt.

As he watched, he felt very left out. Everyone else was star-shaped and beautifully shiny. They were all quick and bright and made him feel very slow and dull. He was so different! Perhaps he'd make an excuse and go home.

But then he noticed that Spangle's friends weren't all the same. That one had six points, not five like Spangle, and this one had silvery spots on her. That one had zig-zag edges, and this one had wavy stripes. He grew more and more interested and was quite surprised when the game finished. Then everybody wanted to meet him and he felt very proud when Spangle said, "This is Fog. He's my best friend."

Everyone insisted that Fog joined in the next game.

"It's Hunt the Grumble," said Spangle.

"What's a Grumble?" asked Fog. He thought he ought to know what he was looking for.

"It's something that's not sparkly and shiny," said Twinkly.

"Oh, I hope that's not me," said Fog, looking down at his green fur. Everybody laughed.

"Fog, you are never dull," said Spangle. "No, you'll recognise the Grumble when you see it."

Everyone rushed off to hunt around the house, and Fog went with them. Everything shone! It was obviously going to be very difficult to find anything that hadn't been decorated with glitter dust for the party.

Fog was so excited he tripped over the corner of the mat (it had ten corners) and underneath he found a little pile of ordinary dust. It didn't glitter a bit!

"I've found it!" he called. "I've found the Grumble!"

"Well done, Fog," said Spangle "and now it's time for tea and presents."

Spangle opened all the star-shaped presents first. There was a cushion covered in sequins, a notebook where the pages sparkled as you wrote on them, a star-shaped balloon that floated up to the ceiling, and a radio tuned into the Milky Way band.

When Fog gave Spangle his present he was still feeling a bit shy about it, but Spangle was delighted.

"A round present!" he exclaimed. "How lovely to have something different!" And Fog thought of all the days to come when he and Spangle would have fun playing together with Spangle's new ball.

In the Bible there are lots of stories about people who were different in some way, or who felt unhappy or left out. Jesus was always careful to show that being different doesn't matter, because God loves everyone. One day Jesus met a small man who was a greedy cheat. He showed Zacchaeus that being short didn't matter at all – and he helped him to stop being greedy and cheating people. You can read how Zacchaeus met Jesus in Luke chapter 19, verses 1 to 10.

Thank you, Jesus that it doesn't
matter what I look like and whether
I am different from other people.
What is important is that you love
me very, very much!

Isn't it beautiful?

Spangle peered through the letter box. What was Fog up to? Spangle knew Fog was in there, but he hadn't answered his knock.

"Fog?" called Spangle. "Please come and open the door."

"I can't," said Fog, "my hands are all sticky and painty. You'll have to find a way in yourself."

Spangle went all the way around the house, but no windows were open. "There's nothing else for it," he said to himself, and zoomed up to the roof. Oh good, there was no smoke coming out of the chimney!

Spangle squeezed himself as thin as he could and slid like a beam of light down the chimney. Fog looked up at the sudden flash.

"Hello, Spangle, it's good to see you."

"Well, I can hardly see you, Fog," replied

Spangle. It was true. Fog was almost hidden by a mound of cardboard tubes, coloured paper, pots of paint, balls of wool and all sorts of sparkly things. He had bits of card stuck all over his fur, and his paws were rainbow-coloured.

Spangle hovered in the fireplace because there was no space on the floor except the little spot where Fog was sitting.

"What are you doing?" Spangle asked.

"I'm making something," said Fog.

"Yes, but what?" persisted Spangle.

"Er... I'm not sure yet," said Fog. "Pass me that red shiny ribbon, would you please, Spangle?"

Spangle put the ribbon on the end of a long tube and held it out to Fog. Fog could just reach it. He looked at it for quite a while before he glued it round and round a small box.

"I think I'll come back later, Fog," said Spangle.

"OK," said Fog, concentrating on picking up a fat paintbrush full of blue paint. Spangle disappeared back up the chimney.

Much later Spangle went back to Fog's house. Outside were three big black plastic bags full of rubbish. Inside was a...

"What is it, Fog?" asked Spangle.

"I'm still not sure," answered Fog, "but isn't it beautiful? I really enjoyed making it!"

Spangle looked at the wonderful collection of boxes and tubes all covered with brilliant colours and sparkles.

"Wow, yes!" said Spangle. "Isn't it beautiful!"

"That's it!" exclaimed Fog. "It's an 'Isn't It Beautiful?' and I love it!"

"It's the best 'Isn't It Beautiful?' in the whole world," said Spangle, "and I love it too."

Have you ever wondered what fun God must have had making the world? What a lot of care he took to get everything just right – the sky, land and sea, and all the creatures who live in them! And when he had finished, he was very pleased. You can read about it in Genesis chapter 1 to chapter 2, verse 4.

Have a think about what you like best of all the things God has made. Could you say, "Isn't It Beautiful" about it? Say thank you to God for all the lovely things you enjoy about his world.

You could say this prayer.

Thank you, God, for your lovely world. I'm so glad you made… and… You are so clever God!

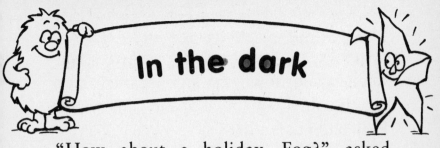

In the dark

"How about a holiday, Fog?" asked Spangle. "My friend the Milky Way Kid has said we can stay in her country cottage."

"Oh great!" said Fog. "When shall we go?"

"First thing in the morning," said Spangle. "Will you be ready?"

Fog spent the rest of the day packing and remembering to tell his neighbours where he was going.

"It's right out in the country, away from everywhere – except the seaside! It's got its own beach!"

The neighbours were impressed!

Fog and Spangle drove off the next day. The cottage was lovely, and all ready for them. The Milky Way Kid had left the key under a flower pot in the garden, and when they got inside they found a supply of food, and a bedroom with two cosy beds.

After a quick lunch, Fog and Spangle went out and explored the garden. Then they walked down the stony path to the little beach. They stared at the wide water. They hadn't seen the sea very often.

"It's a very special place," whispered Fog.

At last they had to leave the beach and go back to the house for supper. It was beginning to get dark, and soon it got very dark indeed. Fog was used to one or two street lights, but there weren't any here! Spangle always made his own light, so he

didn't notice the dark. Fog was glad of the firelight in the cottage as they ate a cosy supper.

"Time for bed, I think," said Spangle, yawning. "I can't wait for tomorrow to come. Lots more fun on the beach!"

"Yes," said Fog, snuggling down under his quilt. "I'm nearly asleep already."

But suddenly Fog wasn't asleep at all. He was wide awake, but in a strange bed, in a strange place, with little noises he didn't recognise. Really, they were just ordinary house noises, but because they were a little bit different from the ones in Fog's own house, he was scared. And he couldn't see anything. It was so dark! Fog had never known such blackness.

Fog remembered where he was and looked over to Spangle's bed. There wasn't a sign of light there. This was because Spangle was asleep under the quilt, but it made Fog even more scared. He shivered and shook in his bed. I'm all alone in the dark, he thought. At last he could bear it no longer. He sat up and shouted, "HELP!"

At once there was a light in the room as

Spangle sat up too. "What's the matter?" he asked sleepily.

"Oh Spangle, I've been so frightened," sobbed Fog. "I was all alone in the dark, and I don't like the dark!"

Spangle gave Fog a cuddle. "It's all right now," he assured him. "But just because you couldn't see me, it didn't mean I wasn't there."

"Oh, I never thought of that," said Fog. "Of course you were there all the time. If I wake up again, I'll remember you're here even if there's no light showing. Oh, I'm tired now! Goodnight again." And he fell asleep straightaway, leaving Spangle wide awake. But as night was Spangle's favourite time, he didn't mind a bit.

There is a story in the Bible where Jesus' friends were frightened. There was a storm at sea. Jesus was with them, asleep in the boat, so they were quite safe really, but they were still frightened until Jesus told the storm to stop. They were amazed to think that Jesus was in charge of the weather! You can read the story in Mark chapter 4, verses 35 to 41.

Perhaps you are frightened sometimes. Remember, Jesus is with you even though you can't see him!

You could say this prayer.

Thank you, Jesus, that you are always with me. Help me to remember this, especially when I am frightened.

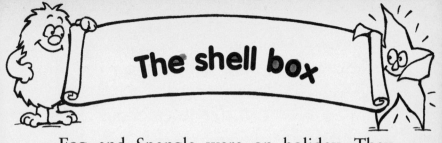

The shell box

Fog and Spangle were on holiday. They were staying in a little cottage by the sea. It was far away from any other house. They could see the nearest one if they looked out of the bedroom window. It was along the coast, standing high on a cliff.

"I wonder who lives there," said Spangle.

"Perhaps we'll meet them one day," said Fog.

Every day Fog and Spangle explored a new place, and every evening they sat by the cosy fire and talked about what fun they had had. One day they found a little beach covered in seashells. Spangle was delighted.

"They're so pretty!" he exclaimed, and Fog helped him to collect some of the nicest ones.

"I love the colours," said Spangle. "I want to keep these shells for ever." They had quite a bagful when they went back to the cottage that evening.

The next day Fog and Spangle had a surprise. It was raining! It had been fine for so long they had forgotten about bad weather.

"Let's stay in," said Fog. "The cottage

could do with a tidy up, and I can make soup for lunch."

"That sounds lovely," said Spangle. "If you don't mind, I think I'll sort my beautiful shells."

Spangle spread the shells out on the table. First he sorted them into sizes, then he sorted them into shapes, and then colours. Then he began to make them into patterns. Suddenly he had an idea. He rummaged through the waste-paper basket.

"Hey!" said Fog. "I've just tidied that all away!"

"I know," said Spangle. "I'm just looking for an empty chocolate box."

He found one. Fortunately the box wasn't squashed. Spangle took it to the table and began arranging the shells on the top. When he had decided on a good pattern, he stuck them down.

"That is beautiful," said Fog, coming in with the hot soup.

"I'm very pleased with it," said Spangle. "I shall keep it as my special treasure box."

As they ate their lunch, they noticed it had stopped raining, so they decided to go for a walk.

"Let's go along to the cliffs," said Spangle. "We haven't been that way yet."

They walked along the beach to where the high cliffs were. The tide was far out, and there were lots of interesting rock pools to explore. Spangle liked looking at the starfish, and Fog was fascinated by the little shrimps darting about. They were so busy they didn't notice the sea creeping nearer as the tide came in. When they looked up, the way back along the beach was covered in water, and there was just the high cliff behind them.

"How are we going to get back?" whispered Fog. "I can't swim very well."

Suddenly they heard a shout. It came from the top of the cliff.

"Look along to the left," shouted a lady. "There are some steps."

Fog and Spangle hunted along the cliff and found a narrow opening with some steps leading upwards. They started to climb.

"Keep going!" shouted the lady. "I'm coming to help you."

It was a long way up the cliff. Fog and Spangle were quite tired when the lady appeared just ahead of them.

"You're nearly there," she said encouragingly. "There are one or two tricky bits I'll help you over."

At last all three were safe at the top of the

cliff by the lady's house. It was the one they had seen from their bedroom. They were meeting the owner sooner than they thought!

"My name's Topsy – Topsy Cliff," she said. "After your adventure I think you need to come in for a cup of seaweed tea!"

Fog and Spangle had a lot to think about that evening as they sat by the fire.

"What a good job Topsy saw us in trouble," said Fog.

"Yes," said Spangle, "and I've decided I'm going to give her my very special shell box. She rescued us, and I want to say a very special 'thank you'."

Spangle gave something precious to Topsy to say thank you to her. In the Bible there is a story about a lady who wanted to say a very special thank you to Jesus. She had a bottle of very expensive perfume, and she poured it all over his head! Some people were cross and thought it was a waste of money, but Jesus knew she did it because she loved him. And everyone must have enjoyed the wonderful scent! You can read the story in Mark chapter 14, verses 3 to 9.

It's good to say thank you to people in special ways. God likes us to say thank you to him too. See if you can think of ten things to thank God for – one for each finger!

Thank you, God, for all you have given me.

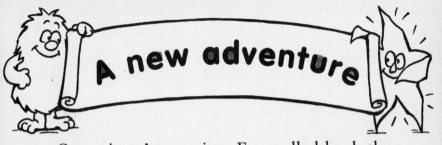

A new adventure

One winter's morning, Fog pulled back the curtains and had quite a shock. The garden had disappeared! There were some lumps and bumps where the rose bushes were, but otherwise everything was flat – and white.

"Snow!" shouted Fog out loud. "Hooray! Snow!"

He rang Spangle even before he had his breakfast.

"Is it snowy where you are, Spangle?" he asked.

"Of course it is," said Spangle. "I'm only three streets away. I'll be round after breakfast, and we can build a snowman in your garden."

Fog put on Wellington boots to keep his feet dry. He didn't need a coat because of his fur, but he wore the bobble hat Auntie Snow had made him. He went out into the garden to start the snowman. Spangle arrived wearing gloves. He didn't really need them, because his sparkle kept him warm. In fact, he had to be careful not to get too excited or he began to melt all the snow around him! But the gloves were bright red and looked good against his yellow sparkle.

They made a beautiful snowman in the garden. They built him near the gate.

"Then he can warn people that the path might be slippery," said Fog. They gave him an icicle nose and pebble eyes and mouth. They found some tinsel from Christmas and made him some hair. He looked splendid!

"Time for lunch," said Fog. "Come inside, Spangle, and I'll cook something hot."

"No, it's all right," said Spangle. "I need to go home and fetch something. I'll be back later."

Fog dried out his fur by the fire as he ate lunch, and wondered what Spangle had gone to fetch.

Spangle came back as quickly as he could, dragging a sledge behind him.

"I made it at woodwork classes," he said proudly. Fog was impressed.

They took turns at pulling each other round the garden, and it was great fun. Then Spangle said, "Let's go up to Mounty Hill. It will be much better there."

"Isn't Mounty Hill a bit steep?" said Fog.

"All the more fun!" said Spangle. "Come on!"

The two friends went along to Mounty Hill. It was in a big park at the edge of town. Mounty Hill was a long steep slope, where people picnicked and flew kites in the summer. Today it was covered in snow, and people were whizzing down on it with sledges and skis.

"They're going awfully fast," said Fog nervously.

"All the more fun!" said Spangle. "Come on!"

At the top of the slope Fog got even more nervous. It was such a long way down!

"I've never done this before," he said. "It looks scary, but it looks fun too."

"Come with me," said Spangle. "We'll go together."

Spangle got on the sledge and Fog sat behind him.

"Ready?" shouted Spangle. "Off we go!"

They pushed with their feet, and whoosh! They rushed down the slope as fast as the wind, and tumbled into the soft snow at the bottom.

"That was great!" said Fog. "Let's do it again!"

Later, as they dried off in front off the fire, Fog said, "Doing new things can be very scary, but it's exciting too. I'm so glad I was brave enough to go sledging down Mounty Hill!"

Lots of people in the Bible found they were doing exciting new things for God. Simon was a fisherman. He was used to going out in a boat, catching fish, but one day Jesus called him to go fishing for people! What he meant was to tell people God's good news, and to help them to live in his kingdom. You can read about it in Mark chapter 1, verses 16 to 18.

To Simon, changing his job must have seemed strange and sometimes difficult, but Jesus was with him, helping and teaching him. Jesus even gave him a new name – Peter!

Sometimes we have new and exciting things to do. It's good to know that Jesus is with us too, helping us when something is strange or difficult.

You could say this prayer.

Help me, Jesus, when I have new and exciting things to do, because sometimes I am a bit scared. Thank you that you are always with me.

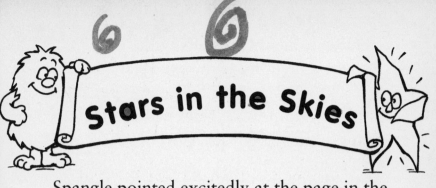

Stars in the Skies

Spangle pointed excitedly at the page in the newspaper.

"Look, Fog! It's the Stars in the Skies contest the night after tomorrow. I'm going in for it. You will come and watch, won't you?"

"I wouldn't miss such a star-studded event for anything," Fog assured Spangle. "What are you going to do?"

"I've been practising my double super-lit dive," said Spangle. "I can do it so fast, I get red and green lights as well as yellow ones."

"It sounds wonderful," said Fog, "but do take care. I know how dangerous star dives can be."

"Oh, I'm very careful," said Spangle.

The Stars in the Skies contest took place on a beautifully clear night. Everybody could see the stars perfectly. First came the children's fancy dress. Fog and Spangle were delighted to see the little stars dressed up as spacemen, rockets and clowns. One family grouped together to make a beautiful flower garden. Lots of prizes were given out, as everyone clapped and cheered.

The next round was the shooting star races. Each group of stars lined up at one side of the sky, and whizzed as fast as they could to the other. Spangle's cousin Twinkly came first in his race.

"Well done, Twinkly!" called Spangle.

"Now it's your turn," said Fog. "All the best, Spangle, and be careful!"

The stars performed one at a time at star diving, so that everyone could see clearly. Spangle watched his friend Dazzler's amazing trick as he waited for his turn.

I've got to be very good to beat that, he thought, but I'm certainly going to try.

"Spangle!" called the referee. Spangle went forward and started his trick, but oh dear! Another star, called Bangle, thought his name had been called, and he started at the same time. The two stars crashed together and fell to the ground. The contest was over for Spangle and Bangle. They both ended up with very bruised points.

Fog was horrified at Spangle's accident. He went straight home with Spangle and helped him to bed. He called the doctor who came and bandaged Spangle, and suggested some ointment Spangle could use.

"How can I get that?" asked Spangle grumpily.

"I'll go," said Fog. "You have a snooze."

Fog went to the chemist to collect the ointment, then he bought some of Spangle's favourite food from the supermarket.

Spangle was still asleep when he got back, so he cooked the meal and waited for him to wake up. Soon he heard groans coming from the bedroom.

"I'm so sore, Fog," said Spangle.

"It's all right, I've got the ointment," said Fog, and he rubbed some gently into Spangle's bruises with his soft paws.

"That feels better," said Spangle. "Ooh, I'm hungry!"

"Here's your dinner – Glitter Crunch pie," said Fog, bringing in a tray. "Let me help you. I don't think you can manage a knife and fork."

Fog fed Spangle using a spoon, and Spangle ate up every delicious scrap.

"Mmm, that was lovely," said Spangle. "I think I'll go back to sleep now."

Fog stayed at Spangle's house for a week while Spangle got better. He did the cooking and the cleaning, and helped in every way he could. Spangle was so grateful to have a friend like Fog.

When Spangle could get up again, Fog said, "I've got something you might like to see – or you might not."

"What is it?" asked Spangle.

"It's a video of the Stars in the Skies contest – and you're on it!"

"Oh yes, I must see that," said Spangle.

They watched it together and loved seeing all the brilliant events. Spangle closed his eyes at the bit where he fell, but he said, "It's a shame I didn't win a prize – but I will next year!"

Fog was just the right sort of person to have around when Spangle was in trouble. He helped in any way he could.

There are lots of stories in the Bible of people helping each other. One of them is in 1 Kings chapter 17, verses 8 to 16, where a woman looks after the prophet Elijah, even though she is poor herself. They both find that God makes sure they don't go hungry, as the little bit of food they have lasts just as long as it needs to!

We never know when we are going to have the chance to help somebody else. The important thing is to be ready and willing whenever it happens, just like Fog was.

You could say this prayer.

Please God, help me to be ready to help other people whenever I can.

Fog's pet ladybird

Fog had found a ladybird in his garden. He had seen lots of ladybirds before, but somehow this one seemed a shinier red than the others, with darker, richer spots. He put out his finger and it crawled up his arm with tiny tickling feet.

I must look after this ladybird, thought Fog. I'll make a nice little house and have it for a pet.

He found an empty jam jar and put some twigs inside it. Then he carefully put the ladybird inside. He made a lid for the jar out of a piece of paper with holes in it, and fixed it on with an elastic band. He made a label saying "Lizzie Ladybird's House". He got out his felt pens and drew ladybirds all round the edge. It really looked splendid.

"Spangle, I've got a pet," said Fog over the phone. "You must come and see her." Spangle came straight away. He was very impressed with Lizzie, and he and Fog discussed how Fog ought to care for her.

"Her house will need to be cleaned out every day," said Spangle.

"Yes, and I'll put fresh twigs in with plenty of greenfly," said Fog, "and animals must have water. I'll put in the lid from my toothpaste tube. That will make a nice little pot for water. And then I mustn't forget exercise. Pets need exercise, you know."

Spangle couldn't believe that Fog would give Lizzie exercise until one morning he met him in the park with Lizzie on a tiny

lead made of cotton thread. Fog was holding the other end of the lead tightly. "It's rather fun coming out with her," said Fog, "because sometimes she flies on her lead like a tiny kite."

Spangle went back to Fog's for tea. They watched Lizzie crawling around in her jam jar while they ate their sandwiches.

"She's a lovely pet," said Spangle.

"Yes," said Fog. "She doesn't talk to me, but she's my best friend next to you."

Two days later Spangle had a phone call. When he picked up the receiver there was just a strange snuffling noise and the sound of water dripping.

"Fog, is that you?" he asked anxiously. The snuffling sounded again. "I'm coming round," said Spangle.

He found Fog crying his eyes out and with very wet fur. Fog couldn't say anything but just pointed to Lizzie's jar which was on its side with the lid off. Spangle knew at once what had happened. Lizzie had flown away. Fog would probably never see her again. He put his arm round Fog and didn't say anything for a long time.

At last Fog felt able to speak. "She was my nearly best friend," he said, "and now she's flown away for ever."

"I know," whispered Spangle. He didn't say, "There are plenty of other ladybirds", or, "Perhaps she's happier in the garden", because he didn't think that would help. He just hugged Fog a bit tighter and later said, "I'll put the kettle on. I'll make a nice pot of starfruit tea."

There are lots of sad stories in the Bible, but God is always there to help people. Jesus' friend Peter said in one of his letters: "God cares for you, so turn all your worries over to him." (1 Peter chapter 5, verse 7)

Jesus met many sad people. One day he met a lady whose son had died. He felt really upset for her, and helped her by bringing the young man back to life. You can read the story in Luke chapter 7, verses 11 to 15.

Jesus knew what it was like to be sad. Just when he needed his friends most, they all ran away. And when they needed him most, but thought he was dead, they found he was alive and with them for ever!

You can talk to God about whatever makes you sad.

He will forgive you if you have done something wrong.

He will be close to you if you are lonely.

He will comfort you if you need a friend.

You could say this prayer.

Thank you, God, that you understand how I feel when I am sad.

Fizzler on the roof

One morning, Spangle received a postcard.
"That's a very interesting looking card,"
said Bertie the postman as he handed it
over. "Is it from somebody special?"

"It's from my cousins, the Fizzlers," said
Spangle. "Stars always send cards with

holes in them. It lets the air get through when they reach the earth's atmosphere."

"Yes, but star shaped holes are particularly special," said Bertie.

Spangle wasn't listening. He was reading the card.

"Oh goody!" he exclaimed. "The Fizzlers are making a visit to earth soon. They come every now and then, you know, and they always land on somebody's roof."

"I've heard of that," said Bertie. "People say it's very special to have a Fizzler on the roof."

"That's right," Spangle said excitedly. "Oh, they're coming next week! I must get everything ready."

Spangle was so busy that he hardly had time to see Fog, but they kept in touch by telephone. Fog was busy too. He had decided to decorate his sitting room with new wallpaper and curtains, and it was taking longer than he expected.

"It's going to look lovely, though, Spangle," he said. "You must come and see it when it's finished."

"So when do these Fizzlers of yours

arrive?" asked Bertie the postman, the following week.

"Tomorrow," said Spangle, "and I shall take them straight round to meet my friend Fog."

"Oh, I don't think you'd better do that," said Bertie. "He's far too busy. I've just delivered a parcel of new paintbrushes to him. He'll be up to his eyes in pots of paint for a few days yet."

Fog looked round his sitting room. It was in a mess! The painting was done at last, and he had almost finished covering the paint marks he had made on the wall by mistake, with a very pretty wallpaper. But he had all the paint pots to get rid of, and the brushes to clean, and even when he tidied up there were the curtains to make. How would he get it all done before Spangle brought his famous Fizzler cousins round tomorrow?

"I know," he thought, "I'll finish the wallpaper, and tidy everything up. Then I'll put up the old curtains again for the time being." So he did, and everything looked neat and tidy as he waited for Spangle and the Fizzlers to arrive.

But they didn't come. Fog waited and waited.

"Where can they be?" wondered Fog.

He went to the front door and looked out along the road. Nobody was in sight except Bertie on his way home from work.

"Have you seen Spangle and his cousins, Bertie?" asked Fog. "I've been expecting them to come all morning."

"Oh dear," said Bertie. "I told Spangle you were too busy to see them."

Fog was very cross. "Too busy? Too busy to see my best friend?" he shouted. And then he saw poor Bertie's face. He was looking very upset. Bertie had only meant to be helpful.

"I'm sorry, Bertie," said Fog. "I didn't mean to shout."

"I'm sorry too," said Bertie. "Let me ring Spangle straightaway and tell him he can come round to see you any time."

Later in the evening they all sat in the garden while the little Fizzlers danced in the moonlight. Little Flick Fizzler came and tapped Fog on the arm.

"Please Mr Fog, can we show you our speshi... speshi..."

"Speciality," whispered Spangle.

"Speshisality," said Flick.

"Oh, yes please," said Fog. He watched delightedly as all the Fizzlers whizzed up to the roof and arranged themselves to make the words "Hello Mr Fog"!

"Oh, Spangle!" said Fog. "It's made me feel so special to have Fizzlers on my roof!"

Poor Bertie! He was only trying to be helpful to Fog, because he knew he was so busy. But he got things very wrong!

Jesus' friends got it wrong one day, too. They thought Jesus was too tired or too busy to see a group of children. They tried to send them away. Jesus was very cross when he found out. Of course he wanted to see the children – and he did see them too! You can read about it in Mark chapter 10, verses 13 to 16.

The story reminds us that all children are very special to Jesus – that means you too!

Thank you, Jesus, that I am special to you.

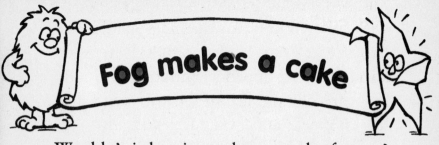

Fog makes a cake

Wouldn't it be nice to have a cake for tea? thought Fog, looking at the picture in the magazine. I think I'll try making one.

Fog had never made a cake on his own before but he thought he knew all about it. He looked at the words in the recipe beside the picture, but as he found it hard to read, he soon gave up and put the book back on the shelf. I know I need eggs, he thought, and flour and butter and sugar. I'll just mix them together, put it in a tin and cook it. It's easy!

It was easy. In fact, breaking the eggs was too easy. One fell on the floor and broke by itself! After he'd cleared it up and wiped his fur, Fog found the flour (would it be the red packet or the blue packet? Oh, the flour inside looked the same. The red packet would do...) and mixed it with the butter and the eggs. Now he needed sugar. He found a packet with a label that started with "S". Inside was something that looked like sugar. Four big spoonfuls were soon stirred in. Fog tipped the mixture into a tin and carefully put it into the hot oven. Then he sat back and waited, licking his lips hungrily.

An interesting smell began to waft through the kitchen as the doorbell rang.

"Hello Spangle!" said Fog. "You're just in time to have a piece of my cake for tea. Come and watch me take it out of the oven." They went into the kitchen, and Spangle watched as Fog put on thick mittens and carefully lifted the hot tin out of the oven.

Something didn't look quite right. The cake was rather flat and a bit too brown. Still perhaps it would taste better than it looked. Fog cut a piece for Spangle and one for himself.

Fog tasted the cake rather carefully, which was just as well because it tasted horrible. Spangle was trying to be polite, but that was rather difficult, so he gave up eating and instead asked, "What did the recipe tell you to put in the cake?"

"Oh," said Fog, "I can't read very well."
He showed Spangle what he had used.

"But that's the wrong sort of flour," said
Spangle. "And this packet says "salt" not
"sugar". No wonder the cake tasted
horrible. I'm not much good at cooking,
but I can see you need some help to get it
right, Fog."

They took the recipe book down from the
shelf and read the recipe through together
carefully. This time they made sure they

had all the right ingredients. Soon the old cake was in the bin and a lovely new one was baking in the oven.

"Thank you for helping me and showing me the right way, Spangle," said Fog.

"Any time," replied Spangle.

"And do you know what," said Fog. "I'm always going to read the recipe in future and cook things properly!"

"You do that, Fog," said Spangle. "Now let's have a piece of good cake!" And they both laughed.

Fog wasn't very good at cooking, was he? But Spangle helped him to understand what to do, and when Fog did things the right way he became a very good cook indeed.

Sometimes we need help to understand things, especially some of the things in God's book, the Bible. An African man was trying to understand something he was reading from the Bible. God sent a man called Philip to explain to him what it meant. You can read about Philip and the man from Ethiopia, in Africa, in Acts chapter 8, verses 26 to 39.

You could say this prayer.

Thank you, God, for all the people who help me to understand your book, the Bible.

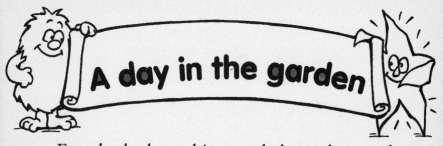

A day in the garden

Fog looked at his tangled garden and thought, "I really must spend some time out here today. I wonder if Spangle could come and help me."

"I'll come as soon as I can," said Spangle over the phone, and sure enough he did, pushing a wheelbarrow laden with a gardening fork, some shears and a trowel.

"Oh good, they'll be useful," said Fog. "As you can see, there's lots to do."

Spangle looked at Fog. He had bits of twig and leaves in his fur, and he seemed to be caught up in a rather thorny hedge. "Are you having a problem, Fog? Perhaps I'd better do the hedge trimming. I haven't got fur to get tangled up in it like you have."

"Oh thank you, Spangle," said Fog, pulling the branches away gingerly. "You've no idea how difficult it is – oops, now I'm caught that side!"

Spangle helped Fog to untangle himself from the hedge. "You go and cut the grass over there," he said. "It's so long, you can hardly see the flowers behind it."

Fog left Spangle to cut the hedge, and went over to what was supposed to be the lawn. Oh dear, he hadn't cut it for weeks, and now it was really hard work. The lawn mower got stuck on such tough grass, so Fog chopped away with Spangle's sharp shears.

Suddenly ahead of him he saw some lovely bright colours. He had worked right across the lawn and reached the flower border the other side. There were a lot of weeds in it, but in amongst them were some gloriously bright orange roses. "Oh, wonderful!" smiled Fog. He went nearer and gave a sniff. What a beautiful perfume! Fog stood and stared at them in wonder.

"Hey!" shouted Spangle. "Why have you stopped work? There's lots more grass to cut."

"I've just found these lovely flowers. Come and look, Spangle. They smell beautiful too."

Spangle agreed that the roses were gorgeous. "But," he said practically, "we've still got lots of work to do. We can enjoy the flowers later."

"Yes we can," thought Fog. "I can put them in the house to enjoy even more." He picked up the shears again and snipped off three of the roses. "I'll put them in water when I've finished this."

Fog carried on with cutting the grass, snip, snip, snip. It was really hard work. His arms ached and it took him much longer than he thought it would. Spangle finished making the hedge tidy, and then started to weed the flowerbed.

"Oh, Fog!" he called. "What a shame, three of your lovely roses have broken off."

"No, they haven't," said Fog. "I picked those. I'm going to put them in the house."

"But Fog, they're all floppy now. I think they are dead."

Fog looked sadly at the roses. Spangle was right. If only he hadn't picked them so soon, or had put them in water straight away. They couldn't survive just cut off from the bush.

"I'll leave the others growing, I think," said Fog. "And thank you, Spangle, for all your hard work. The garden looks lovely! It's time to get the deckchairs out and sit in the sunshine!"

Fog's roses died because they were cut off from the main plant. In the Bible, Jesus used a plant (but not a rose bush) as a picture of himself. He described himself as a vine which would grow sweet juicy grapes. He imagined all his friends (that includes you and me!) as the branches of the vine. If they were cut off, they wouldn't grow. If we don't stay very close to Jesus, we won't grow like him.

You can read about Jesus' picture of the vine in John chapter 15, verses 4 and 5.

Dear Lord Jesus, please help me to stay close to you so that I grow more and more like you.

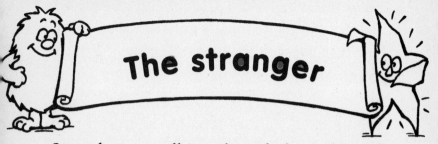

The stranger

Spangle was walking along feeling a bit sad. He had hoped his friend Fog would be able to come out with him, but when he called at Fog's house there was no one there. As he walked along, wondering what he would do by himself all day, he heard a little cough beside him.

"Good morning," said a voice. Spangle looked round to see a stranger beside him. He was very tall and wearing brightly coloured clothes. He had a very happy smiley face.

Spangle was a bit wary. He had been told not to talk to strangers, but there was something about this person that seemed familiar. But no, he definitely hadn't seen him before. However, he didn't want to be rude, so he said "Good morning" back.

"You're looking a bit sad," said the stranger. "Can I help?"

"No, it's all right," said Spangle. "I was hoping to spend the day with my best friend, but he's gone somewhere without me. I think I'll just go home."

"I'm going that way too," said the stranger. (How does he know which way I'm going? thought Spangle.) The stranger's voice sounded a bit muffled, and he was walking in a very wobbly way. Perhaps that bag he was carrying was a bit heavy.

Spangle and the stranger talked as they walked along. He really did seem a nice person, and full of the sort of jokes that

Spangle liked. Perhaps I'll invite him to tea to meet Fog one day, he thought.

Then suddenly the stranger tripped over a stone on the path. He rolled over and two pieces of wood fell out from under his long coat! Then his face fell off! It was a mask, and under it was – Fog!

"I thought I knew you!" exclaimed Spangle. "What are you doing dressed like that?"

"It's a surprise," said Fog. (It certainly was, thought Spangle.) "We're going to a circus fancy dress this afternoon, and I've been to collect our costumes. I'm going to be a clown on stilts – but I need a bit more practice." (You certainly do, thought Spangle.) "Your things are in my bag. You're going to be a juggler."

"Oh no!" said Spangle. "I need to practise too!"

But he was very pleased to see Fog, and what fun they had pretending to be clowns!

Spangle didn't recognise the stranger, although he seemed very familiar. It was a great surprise to discover it was Fog all along!

There is a story in the Bible about some friends of Jesus who didn't recognise him, although he was walking right beside them! He helped them a lot before they realised who he was. You can read about it in Luke chapter 24 verses 13 to 35.

Thank you, Jesus, that I can talk to you at any time, because you are always close to me.

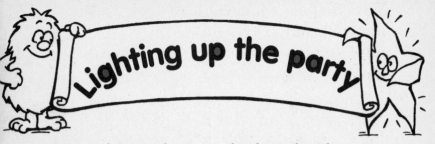

Lighting up the party

Fog and Spangle were thinking hard.

"Such a lot of people are kind to us," said Fog. "I'd like to say thank you to them all. There's the Milky Way Kid, who lent us her holiday cottage."

"There's Bangle who was hurt himself, but sent me a 'get well' card," said Spangle.

"And Bertie, who brings our post," said Fog.

"And Howard who collects the rubbish," said Spangle.

They ended up with a long list. What could they do to say thank you to them all?

"I know!" said Fog. "Let's give a party for all our friends!"

Spangle quickly agreed. He loved parties. But when they began to make plans, he wasn't so sure.

"We can do the food together," said Fog.

"But you're much better at cooking than I

am," said Spangle. "Now you remember to read the recipe book properly!"

"That's true," said Fog, "but you can help me – or do something else."

They went through the list of jobs. Fog seemed to be much better at everything. He ended up being in charge of doing the cooking, making the decorations, writing the invitations *and* wrapping the prizes for the games. Spangle was going to help, of course, but he did wish there was some special thing that he could do.

And then he thought of something. Yes! It was exactly right, and would make the party very special indeed!

"But I thought you were going to help me with the shopping," said Fog, looking at the long list in his paw.

"I will," said Spangle, "but I need to see a few… er… people first. I'm planning a surprise at the party. I'll meet you at the supermarket in time to help carry everything home."

A surprise from Spangle! thought Fog as he walked to the shop. I wonder what he's up to.

Spangle had a big grin on his face when he reached the supermarket.

"It's all arranged," he told Fog.

"What's all arranged?" wondered Fog, but he could see that Spangle wasn't going to give his surprise away, and that he would have to wait for the party to find out what it was.

What a party! Fog's green, orange and yellow decorations looked splendid. All the food was delicious, and everybody had second helpings of the jellybaby trifle. Then they played games. Fog was pleased that

everyone laughed at the jokes hidden in the pass the parcel. At last, after playing musical bumps for the third time, they were all exhausted.

"Time for my surprise," said Spangle. "Come out into the garden, everybody."

By this time it was dark outside. Spangle showed them the garden chairs and rugs he had put out for them to sit on.

"Look up!" he said, then he whizzed out of sight.

As everyone gazed up into the sky, the music started. Then a group of stars appeared, led by Spangle himself. They zoomed and danced in patterns of different shapes. They were joined by hundreds of fireflies, who darted in and out of the shapes in swirly lines. It was wonderful, much better than a firework display. Everyone clapped and cheered, and then sighed as at last the music faded and the stars left the sky.

"Oh, Spangle, what a wonderful end to our party!" said Fog. "How did you think of it?"

"I suddenly remembered the dancing

classes we used to have at Sky School," said Spangle, "so I called all my cousins. It was Twinkly's idea to ask the fireflies to join us."

"Well, I think it was a bright idea," said Fog. "Ho, ho! A very bright idea! Yes, it was certainly bright!" And they both laughed.

Spangle was sad to think he wasn't very clever at some things, but then he thought of something he was good at, and he did that.

Sometimes we might think we can't do anything that's important, but it's good to try our best at what we can do. A lady in the Bible, whose name was Dorcas, was good at sewing clothes, so that is what she did. Everyone was sad when she died, and they cried as they showed Jesus' friend, Peter, the clothes she had made for them. But the story didn't stay sad! God helped Peter to bring Dorcas back to life. You can read about it in Acts chapter 9, verses 36 to 43.

Think about some of the things you can do.

Thank you, God, for all the things I can do. Help me to do them well, especially when I am doing them for other people.

Other books in the *Read to Me* series for you to explore...

Tingling Tums
Margaret Barfield

Meet Sam who learns to ride a bike – without Dad hanging on to the back of it! And Dannielle who discovers she can see in the dark – a secret, shadowy night-time world.

And Jamie who finds a big surprise waiting for him at his new home. Enjoy sharing these stories about the sort of children you would meet on any street or at any school or church. With prayers and poems as well.

ISBN 1 85999 029 0

Keeping up with Grandpa

Janet Slater Bottin

ZZZZZZ-ZIP! ... up went the tent zip. Thomas held tight to Grandpa's hand as they climbed out.
"Grandpa! What's that noise?" he said. "There's something out there!"
Grandpa shone his torch.
Thomas stared into the darkness.
Two bright lights gleamed back!
"Eeeee!" shouted Thomas. "Martians!"

Join Thomas in his adventures with Grandpa: camping, at the farm, starting school...

and the biggest adventure of all – learning more about God.

You can buy these books at your local Christian bookshop or online at
www.scriptureunion.org.uk/publishing
or call Mail Order direct
01908 856006